EXPLORING THE SCIENCE OF NATURE

The Nature and Science of
SHELLS

Jane Burton and Kim Taylor

Gareth Stevens Publishing
MILWAUKEE

For a free color catalog describing Gareth Stevens Publishing's list of high-quality books and multimedia programs, call 1-800-542-2595 (USA) or 1-800-461-9120 (Canada). Gareth Stevens Publishing's Fax: (414) 225-0377.

Library of Congress Cataloging-in-Publication Data

Burton, Jane.
The nature and science of shells / by Jane Burton and Kim Taylor.
p. cm. — (Exploring the science of nature)
Includes bibliographical references and index.
Summary: Discusses shells, what they are made of, their function,
and the creatures that live in them.
ISBN 0-8368-2185-8 (lib. bdg.)
1. Shells—Juvenile literature. 2. Mollusks—Juvenile literature. [1. Shells. 2. Mollusks.]
I. Taylor, Kim. II. Title. III. Series: Burton, Jane. Exploring the science of nature.
QL405.2.B87 1999
591.47'7—dc21 98-45673

First published in North America in 1999 by
Gareth Stevens Publishing
1555 North RiverCenter Drive, Suite 201
Milwaukee, Wisconsin 53212 USA

This U.S. edition © 1999 by Gareth Stevens, Inc. Created with original © 1998 by White Cottage Children's Books. Text © 1998 by Kim Taylor. Photographs © 1998 by Jane Burton, Kim Taylor, and Mark Taylor. The photograph on page 15 (bottom) is by Jan Taylor. Conceived, designed, and produced by White Cottage Children's Books, 29 Lancaster Park, Richmond, Surrey TW10 6AB, England.
Additional end matter © 1999 by Gareth Stevens, Inc.

The rights of Jane Burton and Kim Taylor to be identified as the authors of this work have been asserted by them in accordance with the Copyright, Design and Patents Act 1988. Educational consultant, Jane Weaver; scientific adviser, Dr. Jan Taylor.

Printed in the United States of America

1 2 3 4 5 6 7 8 9 03 02 01 00 99

Contents

Words that appear in the glossary are printed in **boldface** type the first time they occur in the text.

What Shells Do

A shell is a container made of hard material that is specially designed to protect its delicate contents. The hard shell of a snail shields the snail's soft, slimy body from the outside world. The shell of a land snail not only prevents its owner from being injured, it also stops the snail from drying up. In dry places, snails stay moist inside their shells. Slugs, which are like snails without shells, shrivel in dry conditions. Slugs can only live in damp places, but some **species** of snails are able to thrive in deserts.

Snail shells and most other sorts of shells are made of dead material. Once a snail shell forms, it can change shape only by growing along its edge. Compare this with an eggshell. Once an eggshell forms, it does not grow at all. Eggshell is also made of dead material, although the contents of the eggs are very much alive.

Snail shells and eggshells consist mostly of **calcium carbonate**. This is the same chemical of which chalk and limestone hills and mountains in many parts of the world are made. Snail shells can be as hard as stone. They are much less brittle than eggshells because they contain small quantities of materials that eggshells do not have. The materials bind the calcium carbonate together to form a very strong "house" for the snail.

Top, left: A garden snail stays safe and moist inside its shell.

Top, right: The shell of this garden snail is broken, but the snail lives on.

Opposite: The shells of land snails are made of hard, but thin, material. Otherwise, they would be too heavy for their owners to carry.

Below: This edible crab is protected from the outside world by a tough shell. Its shell is really its skin.

Top: Cowries have a special type of coiled shell. The coils are completely hidden inside the shell.

The simplest shape for a shell is the cup shape. Limpet shells are like little upside-down cups. The animal itself lives safely under the cup, holding tightly to a flat rock so that it does not get washed away by waves. Chitons are like limpets, but their shells are more complicated. Eight or more pieces of shell hinge together to form a shallow, oval cup. The animal lives inside the cup. The hinges allow chitons to bend so that they fit snugly into hollows in rocks where **rigid** limpets cannot rest.

Most snail shells are in the form of a coiled tube. The tube gets steadily wider toward the open end. The tube widens to provide more space for the growing snail.

Other types of shells come in two halves, or **valves**, hinged together. These shells are called **bivalves**. Clams are bivalves that bury themselves in sand or mud. Mussels and oysters are bivalves

Right: The purplish black shells of these mussels have to be strong to withstand the pounding of the Pacific Ocean on the western coast of North America.

Above: Waves crash onto the cone-shaped shells of limpets without washing them off the rocks.

A chiton shell is formed of jointed plates so that it can bend as the animal crawls over rocks.

An abalone clings to rocks, like a limpet. Its shell grows in a wide **spiral**.

that fasten themselves to rocks. The two valves of a bivalve shell can be the same shape or they can be different. Scallops have beautiful fan-shaped shells — a flat shell below fits perfectly with a shallow, saucer-shaped shell above.

Many shells are shaped for strength. For instance, an eggshell only has to be strong enough to withstand bumping against other eggs in the nest. It must not be too strong, however, because then a little chick inside could not crack it open to hatch.

Below: The shell of a freshwater red ramshorn snail grows in a flat spiral.

The flame scallop bivalve opens the halves of its shell to breathe and feed.

A queen conch reaches out with a foot to turn its heavy, coiled shell right side up.

Right: The volute is a coiled shell found in the Indo-Pacific.

Above: Some snails have hard shell doors. This turban's shell door has grown in a spiral.

Above: Most snail shells grow in dextral spirals. The shell in the center has been ground away to show its construction.

Right: The animal inside a painted topshell has simple eyes and two feelers for finding its way around.

Many kinds of snails have spiral shells. The spirals can be flat, like clock springs, or they can be pointed, like twisted church spires. However, most snail shells are somewhere in between.

Spiral snail shells can be right-handed, called **dextral**, or left-handed, called **sinistral**. Look at the pointed end of a spiral shell. Starting at the point, follow the coils to see which direction they turn. If they turn clockwise, it is a dextral shell. If they turn counterclockwise, it is sinistral. Most species of snail are dextral, but a few are sinistral. Even within one **genus**, there can be both dextral and sinistral species. Very rarely, a sinistral individual of a dextral species is found. This is a collector's item.

Left: A spirula swims deep in the ocean. Within its body is a thin, coiled shell containing gas. The gas keeps the spirula from sinking.

Below: Serpulid worms make spiral tubes to live in. They "cement" the tubes to rock. These worms do not travel around like snails do.

Snails are not the only creatures to have spiral shells. An octopus-like animal called a nautilus has a very similar type of shell. A nautilus shell is a flat spiral. It is divided into compartments, with the animal itself occupying the large compartment at the end. The other compartments are filled with gas to keep the nautilus afloat in the warm ocean waters where it lives.

Another octopus-like animal, called a spirula, has a thin spiral shell. This shell lies within the animal's body. The spirula shell does not protect the animal. Its purpose is to contain gas and act as a float.

Why did snails **evolve** coiled shells? Coiling is a tidy way of storing a tube. Imagine a snail shell uncoiled and sticking straight out. It would be a long, thin spike and very inconvenient for the animal to carry. Also, a spike-like tube could be easily broken. Coiling the tube and joining the coils together make strong, compact housing.

Snails are not the only animals that live in coiled tubes. Some kinds of **marine** worms build tubes of calcium carbonate, and some of these tubes are coiled. Worm tubes attach to rocks or seaweed. Their owners do not move the shells around like snails do.

Nautiluses probably evolved coiled shells for the same reasons snails did. Nautiluses are related to octopus-like creatures with coiled shells called ammonites. Ammonites lived in the warm oceans 150 million years ago. There are no ammonites alive today, but their shells can still be found by **fossil** hunters.

Opposite: This picture shows a complete shell plus a half-shell of a pearly nautilus. The animal lives in the large section at the end of the shell. The other compartments contain gas that allows the shell to float. When a nautilus wants to sink, it pumps water into the gas-filled compartments.

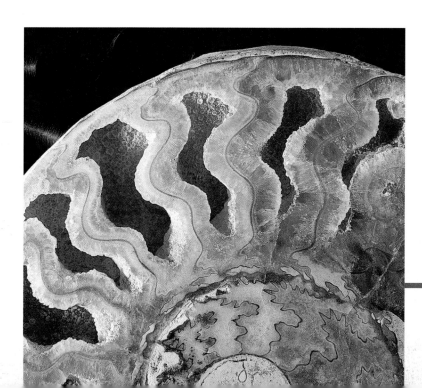

Left: Ammonites, which lived millions of years ago, were similar animals to nautiluses. This fossil shows how an ammonite shell was divided into compartments.

Two Valves

Top: A scallop shell consists of two fan-shaped valves. The valves are hinged along the straight edge at the **apex** of the shell.

Bivalve shells have been around for millions of years. Some fossil bivalves in rocks date back more than 500 million years. From then until the present, a great variety of different shell shapes has evolved. In that time, no bivalve has ever managed to live on land. They all live either in the oceans and seas or in lakes and rivers.

The body of a bivalve resides between the two valves. The valves are joined by a hinge on one side. The hinge may be as simple as a strip of flexible material joining the straight edges of the two valves. Some bivalve shells have ridges and grooves along the hinge. The ridges on one half of the shell fit into the grooves on the other half to strengthen the hinge.

Right: Cockle shells are built of two shallow, cup-shaped valves, hinged to one side of the apex.

Left: Common Caribbean donax shells are wedge shaped. The animal inside extends a long foot to pull its shell over the sand, pointed end first.

Below: The flexible hinge of this common cockle shell is on the right of the apex.

A bivalve shell can be held tightly shut by its owner's strong muscle. This clamping of the two valves of the shell together protects the bivalve from attack. When danger passes, the bivalve relaxes its muscle so that its shell opens slightly. It then extends a pair of tubes called **siphons**, through which it breathes and feeds. Water is drawn in through one tube and pushed out through the other in a steady flow. The animal breathes by extracting oxygen from the water. It feeds by filtering out tiny specks of food material suspended in the water. Large numbers of feeding bivalves can clear muddy water by filtering out all the suspended particles.

In addition to siphons, some bivalves have a muscular foot that they use for pushing or pulling themselves along. Scallops have developed even farther. They can swim for short distances by quickly opening and shutting their shells.

Below: A living cockle extends two siphons to feed and breathe. Growth rings (looking like cracks) curve across the ridges of the shell.

Above: Oysters are not the only bivalves that form pearls. These little pearls formed inside the shell of a horse mussel.

Above: The inside of an abalone shell is smooth and silvery. It displays the rainbow colors of mother-of-pearl.

Right: A pearl oyster is a bivalve. The pearls are made of the same material as the shell itself. They probably formed around grains of sand that became trapped inside the oyster.

The shells of bivalves and the coiled shells of other **mollusks** have three layers. The outer layer is thin and consists of the same flexible material, called **conchiolin**, as the hinge. It does not contain the hard calcium carbonate found in the other two layers.

The middle layer is thick and is built of tiny crystals of calcium carbonate mixed in with thin layers of conchiolin. The middle layer gives the shell strength. The inner layer is similar to the middle layer except that alternate layers of calcium carbonate and conchiolin are **parallel** and very close together. This often gives the inside of the shell the rainbow colors called mother-of-pearl.

Ridges on the outer surface of a bivalve shell show how much the shell has grown each year. They are like the growth rings of a tree. The outer and middle layers of the shell grow only along their edges. At the end of each growth spurt, another ridge forms. The inner layer is laid down continuously throughout the inside of the shell. It is silky smooth to touch.

The shells of bivalves can vary in size from 0.6 inch (15 millimeters) in diameter for the smallest species to 2 feet (60 centimeters) or more in diameter for giant clams. Giant clam shells are so strong that they can be broken only with great effort.

Left: The wavy blue-green flaps mark the edges of a giant clam. Its shell is buried among loose pieces of coral in a tropical lagoon.

Eggshells

Above: A red-legged partridge hatched from this egg.

Right: This baby magpie chipped the top off its egg and hatched.

The shells of mollusks consist of layers of calcium carbonate crystals. The shells of birds' eggs are also made of calcium carbonate, but the crystals are arranged differently. Instead of being arranged in layers, the crystals in an eggshell are arranged in a honeycomb pattern. Each crystal is shaped like a wedge. An eggshell is built of millions of these tiny wedges, each with its narrow end pointing inward and its wide end pointing out.

Pressure on the outside of an egg squeezes the wedges together. Pressure from inside the egg forces them apart. This makes the egg more difficult to break into than out of. This is exactly how an eggshell needs to be. A chick is safe from harm from the outside world. However, it can easily hatch when it is ready.

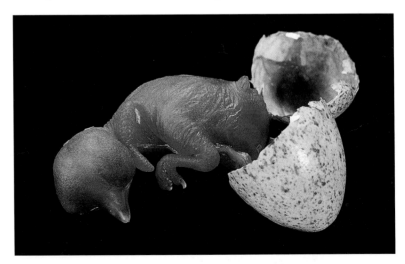

Left: When they are ready to hatch, baby grass snakes cut slits in their leathery eggshells.

Snakes, lizards, and turtles also lay eggs. Their eggs have shells that are leathery and tough, not hard and brittle like the shells of birds' eggs. Dinosaurs, which lived millions of years ago, laid eggs, too. Some small species of dinosaurs ran on their hind legs, looking like wingless birds. Their eggs looked like birds' eggs, and the eggshells had the same arrangement of crystals as birds' eggs. Scientists think birds evolved from dinosaurs.

Above: An egg-eating snake finds a tasty meal in the form of a smooth, white egg.

Below: The unbroken egg seems as though it is stretching the snake's throat uncomfortably.

The snake gets its mouth around the egg by unhinging and stretching its lower jaw.

The snake crushes the egg with spikes inside its throat. It then swallows the egg's contents.

Crab Shells

Top: This may look like a live fiddler crab, but it is not. It is the shell left behind when the crab changed shells.

Above: When a shore crab changes its shell, it comes out of the old shell backward.

Insects, spiders, and crabs do not have skeletons inside their bodies like birds and mammals. Instead, the skeleton is outside the body — like a shell — and is called an **exoskeleton**. Insect exoskeletons are formed of a very strong material called **chitin**. Chitin is not rigid like eggshell. It bends and springs back into shape. It is similar to humanmade plastics that are very strong, but light.

Crab shells are formed partly of chitin, but the chitin is mostly **calcified**. This means it includes calcium carbonate. Calcium carbonate makes crab shells rigid.

The rigid parts of a crab's exoskeleton are hinged together to form **joints**. Legs and claws are

Right: The soft body of an edible crab is bigger than the old shell from which it is emerging.

hinged to the crab's body, and each leg or claw is formed of several hinged sections. At each hinge, there is a small area of thin, uncalcified chitin that bends when the joint is moved. The chitin acts as skin to protect the joint.

A crab shell cannot grow once it has formed, so crabs have to shed their shells in order to grow. The old shell splits, and the crab comes out, covered in a thin, soft skin of flexible chitin. After several days, the crab's new skin calcifies and becomes hard.

Above: A soft, brilliantly colored Pacific lobster moves away from its dull, old shell.

Urchin Shells

Top: The shell of an edible sea urchin is divided into five segments.

Sea urchins are round creatures that do not seem to have a back or a front, although they do have a top and a bottom. They creep along slowly on hundreds of tiny tube feet.

Some urchins have needle-like spines. If a fish swims too near and touches one of the spines, the urchin directs surrounding spines toward it, forming a barrier of needle points for protection.

The thin, brittle shell of a sea urchin consists of many calcium carbonate plates that fit together neatly. Urchin shells are divided into five segments. The segments are separated by rows of tiny holes. The sea urchin controls its tube feet through these holes.

Above: The shell of an East African urchin is covered in rows of little knobs on which its spines hinge.

Right: The tube feet of this purple-tipped sea urchin are clearly visible. The urchin is wearing a limpet shell as a hat.

Above: Some urchins use their spines like legs. This one waves its upper spines while it creeps along on its lower spines.

Above: Sand dollars gradually bury themselves by moving sand grains over their backs with their tiny spines.

The outside of a spiny urchin shell is covered with little polished knobs. The spines of the urchin hinge on these knobs. Sockets in the blunt ends of the spines fit onto the knobs, forming tiny ball-and-socket joints. These allow the spines to move in any direction to ward off enemies.

Flattened sea urchins, called sand dollars, live on sandy shores. They are covered in spines, which aid in movement and burrowing. Sand dollars are slightly curved on top and flat underneath. This special shape allows an upside-down sand dollar to right itself as if by magic. Gentle water movement, caused by waves, gets underneath the curved side of the sand dollar and flips it over. It can then rest firmly, flat side down.

Above: Heart urchins make their homes buried in the sand. Little holes all over the shells show where the animals' tube feet were.

 # Tortoiseshell

Top: When a baby spur-thighed tortoise hatches from its egg, its shell is soft and folded underneath.

Animals with backbones, called **vertebrates**, do not normally have shells. Their bodies are covered with flexible skin, and their bony skeletons are hidden inside. Tortoises and turtles are vertebrates that have a bony skeleton, but they also have a box-like shell. The box has two openings — one at the front for the head and front legs, and one at the back for the tail and hind legs. A tortoise or turtle under attack pulls its legs, head, and tail into its shell for protection.

A tortoise's shell is built of many flat slabs of bone, joined together at their edges. This "box" of bone is covered with a thin layer of skin. Strong, horny plates grow on the outside of the skin, each plate matching the bony slab beneath it. The horny plates have developed from scales, and both are made of the same material, called **keratin**. Hair is also made of keratin.

Right: A hawksbill turtle swims in the ocean. Its shell is streamlined to pass through water smoothly.

22

As the tortoise grows, so do the bone slabs of its shell along their edges. The horny plates above the bone grow in layers. Each new layer is slightly larger than the previous one to keep pace with the bone beneath. The ridges on the outside of a tortoise's shell mark the edges of the horny layers.

Tortoiseshell combs and various ornaments were once made from the plates of sea turtles' shells. Fortunately, in modern times, the turtles are protected.

Above: A large leopard tortoise stumps over the dry African grass. Its shell protects it from attackers, such as eagles and jackals. The photograph was taken with a long exposure, giving the impression of swift movement.

Below: A leopard tortoise can withdraw its legs, head, and tail into its shell.

The underside of a leopard tortoise shows the ridges that formed as the horny plates grew.

Second-hand Shells

Top: Hermit crabs have unprotected abdomens and must live in abandoned shells. This empty triton shell would be a great find for a growing hermit crab.

Shells built by one kind of animal can be used as homes by other kinds of animals, once the original owners no longer need the shells. Spiral seashells of almost any kind, for instance, can be taken over by hermit crabs. These crabs have their own hard shells that cover their legs and claws, but their soft bodies are unprotected. A hermit crab backs into an empty seashell, leaving a specially shaped claw to block the entrance of the shell. Here, the crab is safe from **predators**.

Right: A common octopus has squeezed its soft body and most of its arms into a triton shell home.

Above: A hermit crab feels inside an empty shell to make sure it is the right size and unoccupied.

Quickly, the hermit crab moves its soft body out of its old shell and into a new one.

Unfortunately for hermit crabs, their borrowed homes do not grow. So, as the crab gets bigger, it has to start looking for a bigger home. Most shells on the seashore already have snails or crabs in them so a growing hermit crab is constantly looking for an empty shell. Changing over from one shell to another has to be done quickly, so that the soft parts of the hermit crab are not exposed for more than a few seconds.

On land, empty snail shells are often used as homes by woodlice and spiders. These animals do not move the shells around with them the way hermit crabs do. Some species of small, solitary bees also build their mud nests inside empty snail shells. They cover the shells with bits of grass to keep them from getting too hot in the Sun.

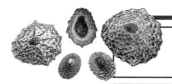

From Shell to Stone

Above: The thick shells of limpets, such as these, are sometimes washed ashore in huge numbers.

Chalk and limestone are made of calcium carbonate, which is the same material as the shells of snails, clams, and some other animals. In fact, chalk is formed from the shells of tiny creatures that lived in the oceans millions of years ago. These animals drifted near the surface of the water, taking **carbon dioxide** from the **atmosphere**. They combined the carbon dioxide with calcium in the water to make their shells. When the animals died, the shells slowly sank to the bottom of the ocean, where they settled in layers, hundreds of feet (meters) thick. The pressure from more and

Right: Layers of slipper limpet and oyster shells are dumped by ocean currents on a beach.

more shells raining down over millions of years turned the lower shell layers into chalk rock. More pressure and heat from within the Earth later turned some of the chalk into limestone.

Even now, the shells of sea snails and clams are turning into rock. The shells gather on some beaches where waves pound them into shell sand. The sand becomes buried, and pressure squeezes it into shell rock.

Humans and all other animals need oxygen to breathe, not carbon dioxide. Thanks are owed to the shelled creatures of the world for taking so much carbon dioxide out of the atmosphere and locking it away in mountains of chalk and limestone. If all the carbon dioxide in these mountains were put back into the atmosphere, humans and other animals could not breathe.

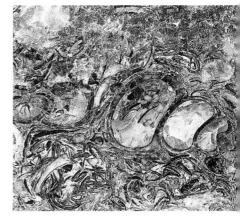

Above: The cut and polished surface of a chunk of sussex marble shows that it consists of the fossilized shells of thousands of freshwater snails.

Left: High chalk cliffs once lay at the bottom of the ocean. They were formed of the shells of countless millions of tiny sea creatures.

Activities:

Shell Collecting

Shells are beautiful objects. When you find one, study its shape and the pattern and colors of its markings. Feel the texture of its surface.

All these things make shells wonderful objects to collect. When starting a shell collection, first find a good place to store the shells. A cabinet with several drawers is ideal. If you have access to a cabinet with a glass front, the beautiful shells you have found will give pleasure to everyone.

Another idea is to arrange the shells on colorful dinner plates. Choose plate colors that will blend tastefully with the colors of your shells. Displaying your shells on top of a mirror is another way to showcase their natural beauty.

The next requirement is a shell field guide that will help you identify the shells you find. Compare your finds with the illustrations in the guide. How many kinds of shells do you have in your collection?

Below: Display your shells on a mirror so you can see both sides at once.

Did you find a garden snail, a crab shell, a lobster shell, a cowrie shell, a mussel shell, a limpet shell, a chiton shell, an abalone shell, a scallop shell, a conch shell, a turban's shell, a painted topshell, a worm shell, a nautilus shell, a cockle shell, a Caribbean donax shell, an oyster shell, a clam shell, a robin's eggshell, a sea urchin shell, a sand dollar, or a triton shell?

Did you find coiled shells, bivalves, and spiral shells?

Write the name of each shell, along with the place and date you found it, on a small square of paper or a label. Keep each name tag with its shell.

You can arrange your collection in several ways. You could divide the shells according to shape and type. Or, if you go regularly to a number of different beaches, you could make collections for each beach. Another way to arrange the shells is by size. What is your largest shell? What is your tiniest shell? Which is your most colorful shell?

Hear the Sea?

At the beach, pick up a large seashell, such as a whelk or conch, and hold it to your ear. Do you hear the hollow, rushing sound of surf on the beach? Take the same shell home and listen to it again. Can you still hear the sound of surf, or something like it? The shell gathers any little sounds and mixes them to make a steady rushing noise, like the sounds of the sea.

on 400-grade sandpaper and polish it on 1000-grade. A final polish with metal polish and a soft cloth will leave the cut surface bright and shiny.

Shell Sections

A coiled seashell is a beautiful object from the outside, but you cannot see its full structure just from that view.

To see the inside, you need to divide the shell into sections. To do this, get various grades of wet/dry sandpaper; a hard, flat surface; and plenty of water. You will also need a lot of energy and patience, since sectioning a shell — especially if it is a big one — is hard work.

Choose a shell that you do not value too much, perhaps because it is slightly broken or worn. Wet a sheet of 240-grade sandpaper and lay it on a hard surface. Rub one side of the shell on the paper until you have ground it flat (*above*). You will need to rinse the paper frequently to wash away the powdered shell.

Continue rubbing until you reach the middle of the shell and the structure of all its whorls is exposed (*below*). You may then want to further smooth the ground surface

Pendants and earrings can be made from shells that have been ground down on both sides to leave a central section 0.1-0.15 inch (3-4 mm) thick. Wear gloves, and be careful when grinding thin sections so that your fingers do not frequently touch the paper. Skin injures easily!

Above: A collection of land snail shells can be displayed in a glass jar.

Glossary

apex: the top point of any triangular or conical shape. The apex is the part of a shell that is first formed.

atmosphere: the layer of air and clouds that surrounds Earth.

bivalves: animals that have shells formed of two separate valves, or halves.

calcified: containing calcium carbonate.

calcium carbonate: a chemical formed of calcium, carbon, and oxygen. Chalk is calcium carbonate.

carbon dioxide: a gas formed of carbon and oxygen. Humans and animals breathe in oxygen and breathe out carbon dioxide. Shelled creatures and plants remove carbon dioxide from the atmosphere.

chitin: a very tough material from which the skin of insects and many other types of animals are formed.

conchiolin: the main material from which the shells of mollusks are formed.

dextral: right-handed; spiraling in a clockwise direction.

evolve: to slowly and gradually advance from one form to another. Over millions of years, plants and animals evolve into new species.

exoskeleton: the hard, supporting skin on the outside of certain animals.

fossil: traces of animal or plant material from an earlier time. Over the passage of millions of years, the material turns to stone.

genus: the name given to a group of similar species. For instance, the large white butterfly (*Pieris brassicae*) and the small white butterfly (*Pieris rapae*) are separate species in the same genus. *Pieris* is the genus name. *Brassicae* and *rapae* are species names.

joint: the point where two or more bones come together.

keratin: the tough material from which hair, fingernails, and horn are formed.

marine: living in the seas or oceans.

mollusks: animals that live in water and usually have a hard, outer shell — including snails and bivalves.

parallel: running side-by-side without getting closer together, farther apart, or touching.

predator: an animal that hunts other animals for food.

rigid: unable to bend.

sinistral: left-handed; spiraling in a counterclockwise direction.

siphon: a tube through which water can flow.

species: a biologically distinct kind of animal or plant. Similar species are grouped into the same genus.

spiral: a continuous line that curves inward or outward, clockwise or counterclockwise, from a central point.

valves: the two halves of a bivalve shell.

vertebrate: an animal with a backbone.

Plants and Animals

The common names of plants and animals vary from language to language. But plants and animals also have scientific names, based on Greek or Latin words, that are the same the world over. Each plant and animal has two scientific names. The first name is called the genus. It starts with a capital letter. The second name is the species name. It starts with a small letter.

abalone (*Haliotis species*) — warm seas worldwide 7, 14

ammonite (*Harpoceras falciferum*) — Europe 11

common Caribbean donax (*Donax denticulatus*) — Caribbean 13

common cockle (*Cardium edule*) — Atlantic 12, 13

common hermit crab (*Eupagurus bernhardus*) — eastern Atlantic 24, 25

common octopus (*Octopus vulgaris*) — Atlantic 24

edible crab (*Cancer pagurus*) — eastern Atlantic 5, 18

egg-eating snake (*Dasypeltis scabra*) — Africa 17

grass snake (*Natrix natrix*) — Europe 17

hawksbill turtle (*Eretmochelys imbricata*) — tropical seas 22

horse mussel (*Modiolus modiolus*) — Eastern Atlantic 14

leopard tortoise (*Testudo pardalis*) — Africa 23

magpie (*Pica pica*) — Europe, North America, Asia 16

Pacific lobster (*Enoplometopus occidentalis*) — Pacific 19

painted topshell (*Calliostoma zizyphinum*) — Eastern Atlantic 8, 15

pearl oyster (*Pinctada species*) — Indo-Pacific 14

pearly nautilus (*Nautilus pompilius*) — Indo-Pacific 10-11

purple-tipped sea urchin (*Psammechinus miliaris*) — Eastern Atlantic 20

queen conch (*Strombus gigas*) — Caribbean 7, 28

sand dollar (*Clypeaster species*) — warm seas worldwide 21

serpulid worm (*Rotalaria concava*) — Europe 9

Books to Read

The Horseshoe Crab. Nancy Day (Silver Burdett)
Invertebrates. Alvin Silverstein (TFC)
Seashells. R. Tucker Abbot (Thunder Bay)
Seashells, Crabs, and Sea Stars. *Young Naturalist Field Guides (series)*. C. Kump Tibbitts (Gareth Stevens)
Shell. Alex Arthur (Knopf)

The Shell Book. Barbara Hirsch Lember (Houghton Mifflin)
Shells. Jennifer Coldrey (Dorling Kindersley)
What Lives In a Shell? Kathleen Weidner Zoehfeld (HarperCollins)
What's Under That Shell? D. M. Souze (Lerner Group)

Videos and Web Sites

Videos

The Crab. (Barr Films)
A Nature Walk at Low Tide. (Beacon)
Sea Shell Animals. (Phoenix/BFA)
Shell. (DK Vision)
The Snail. (Barr Films)
Turtles. (Agency for Instructional Technology)
When the Tide Goes Out. (New Dimension)

Web Sites

www.seashells.com/seashells.htm
www.wh.whoi.edu/homepage/faq.html
www.assateague.com/shells.html
lac.laci.net/pweb.erpuig/imagalph.html
www.concentric.net/~Tertou/jltz.html
www.seaworld.org/
www.goals.com/kyrnos/tuamz.htm
www.wcs.org/kids/

Some web sites stay current longer than others. For further web sites, use your search engines to locate the following topics: *ammonites*, *bivalves*, *crabs*, *mollusks*, *pearls*, *seashells*, and *snails*.

Index